Humpty D & MORE

Executive Producers: **Kim Mitzo Thompson, Karen Mitzo Hilderbrand**
Music Arranged By: **Hal Wright**
Music Vocals: **The Nashville Kids Sound**
Illustrated By: **Sharon Lane Holm**
Book Design: **Jennifer Birchler**

Published By:
Twin Sisters Productions
4710 Hudson Drive
Stow, OH 44224 USA
www.twinsisters.com   1-800-248-8946

ISBN-13: 978-159922-506-7

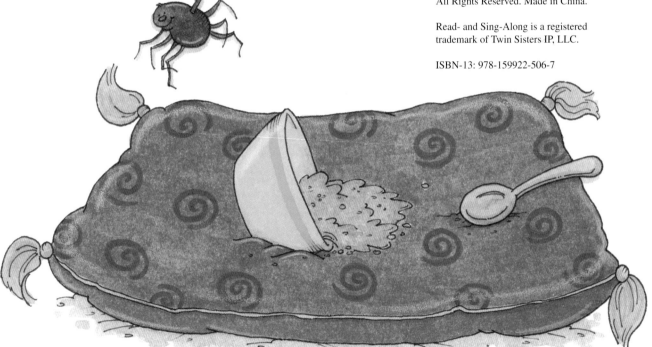

Humpty Dumpty sat on a wall.
Humpty Dumpty had a great fall.
All the king's horses and all the king's men
couldn't put Humpty together again.

So some children came along
singing Humpty's little song.

So they decided to think of a plan
to put Humpty together again.

Working with some glue and tape,
they gave Humpty a new shape.
Now Humpty Dumpty sits on a wall.
Never again will Humpty fall.

Now when Humpty's story is told
a happy ending will unfold.
Working together to help Humpty mend—
working together, they helped a friend.

Jack and Jill went up the hill
to fetch a pail of water.
Jack fell down and broke his crown
and Jill came tumbling after.

Oh where, oh where has my little dog gone?
Oh where, oh where can he be?
With his ears cut short and his tail cut long,
oh where, oh where can he be?

This little pig went to market.

This little pig stayed home.

This little pig had roast beef.

This little pig had none.

This little pig cried,
"Wee-wee-wee," all the way home!

Little Miss Muffet sat on a tuffet
eating her curds and whey.
Along came a spider
and sat down beside her
and frightened Miss Muffet away.

Tell what is happening in each picture. Point to what happened first in the story, next in the story, and then last in the story.